55x3/11

P9-EDE-954

WITHDRAWN

j   c.3
E

VAN LEEUWEN.
  OLIVER AND AMANDA'S CHRISTMAS.

1989   6.97   4-90

Alameda Free Library
Alameda, CA 94501

OLIVER
AND AMANDA'S
CHRISTMAS

Jean Van Leeuwen

PICTURES BY

ANN SCHWENINGER

DIAL BOOKS FOR YOUNG READERS
NEW YORK C.3

ALAMEDA FREE LIBRARY

LEEUWEN

For Bruce and David
and Elizabeth

J.V.L.

For Denise and David
and Indigo

A.S.

Published by Dial Books for Young Readers
A Division of Penguin Books USA Inc.
2 Park Avenue
New York, New York 10016

Published simultaneously in Canada by
Fitzhenry & Whiteside Limited, Toronto

Text copyright © 1989 by Jean Van Leeuwen
Pictures copyright © 1989 by Ann Schweninger
All rights reserved
Printed in Hong Kong by South China Printing Co.

The Dial Easy-to-Read logo is a registered trademark of
Dial Books for Young Readers,
a division of Penguin Books USA Inc., ® TM 1,162,718.

Van Leeuwen, Jean. Oliver and Amanda's Christmas
by Jean Van Leeuwen/Ann Schweninger, illustrator.
p.   cm.
Summary: After joining his sister in wrapping presents,
baking cookies, and picking a Christmas tree, Oliver
tries to find a stocking big enough to hold the
twenty-two toys he requested from Santa.
ISBN 0-8037-0636-7.   ISBN 0-8037-0647-2 (lib. bdg.)
[1. Christmas—Fiction. 2. Brothers
and sisters—Fiction. 3. Pigs—Fiction.]
I. Schweninger, Ann, ill. II. Title.
PZ7.V32730m 1989   [E]—dc19   88-23710   CIP   AC.

First Edition
E
1 3 5 7 9 10 8 6 4 2

The full-color artwork was prepared using carbon pencil,
colored pencils, and watercolor washes. It was then color-separated
and reproduced as red, blue, yellow, and black halftones.

Reading Level 1.9

CONTENTS

SECRETS

Christmas was coming in eight days.

Mother was baking.

Father was shopping.

Oliver and Amanda were writing letters
to Santa.

"Dear Santa," said Amanda's letter.

"I would like a bike

and a baby doll and a paint set.

And anything else you have.

Have a good trip.

Love, Amanda"

Oliver was on the third page

of his letter.

Oliver wanted a lot of things.

Father came in the door,

his arms full of packages.

"What is in that great big box?"

asked Amanda.

"Never mind," said Father.

"*Psst. Psssst,*" he whispered

in Mother's ear.

"What did you say?" asked Amanda.

"Can't tell," said Father.

"It's a secret."

Everyone was having secrets.

Mother's door was closed.

There were strange sounds behind it.

And no one was allowed to look

in the hall closet.

Even Oliver had a secret.

After lunch he went to his room.

Amanda heard banging inside.

What was Oliver doing?

She peeked under the door,

but she couldn't see anything.

The banging stopped.

Oliver opened the door

and stepped on Amanda.

"What are you doing here?" he asked.

"What are you doing in your room?"

asked Amanda.

"Can't you see it's a secret?"

said Oliver. "Go away, Amanda."

Amanda stamped down the hall

to her room and closed the door.

She could have secrets too.

She found a crayon and made a sign.

KEEP OUT. GO AWAY. SECRETS INSIDE.

She put the sign on her door.

Then she sat on her bed and thought.

What could her secrets be?

Amanda thought a long time.

She saw a painting on her wall.

"Mother likes my pictures," she said.

"For Christmas I could make her

a picture of me."

She went to her closet

where she kept a box of junk.

"I could make Father something

to keep his pencils in."

She dumped everything out of the box.

"And I could make Oliver

a parking garage for his cars."

Amanda went to work

with her scissors, glue, and paints.

There was a knock on her door.

"Don't come in," said Amanda.

"Why not?" asked Mother.

"I am busy," said Amanda.

"What are you so busy doing

for hours and hours?" asked Mother.

"Can't tell," said Amanda.

"It's a secret."

THE BEST CHRISTMAS TREE

"Today," said Father, "we are going

to get our Christmas tree."

"Hooray!" shouted Oliver and Amanda.

They put on their coats.

Mother put on her fuzzy hat.

And they all went for a walk

in the woods

to find their Christmas tree.

"I see it!" said Amanda.

"I see our Christmas tree."

"That one is too short," said Oliver.

"I like tall Christmas trees."

They walked some more.
"Here is our Christmas tree,"
said Oliver.

"It is taller even than Father."
"That one is too skinny,"
said Amanda. "I like fat trees."
They kept walking.

"I think this is our Christmas tree," said Oliver.

"It is very tall and very fat."

"I like it," said Amanda.

Mother walked around the tree.

"It is tall," she said.

"And it is fat. But it is crooked. I like a nice straight tree."

They walked and walked.

They saw tall trees and fat trees

and straight trees.

But something was wrong with each one.

"My legs are tired of walking,"

said Amanda.

"My nose is cold," said Oliver.

"Let's stop for a rest," said Father.

They sat down on a fallen log.

Mother poured hot chocolate
for everyone.

"Father," said Amanda.
"What is that round thing
in that tree over there?"

Father looked.

"Why, it is a bird's nest,"

he said. "It is empty.

It must be left over from spring."

"A tree with a nest is nice,"

said Amanda.

"Maybe that is our Christmas tree."

Everyone looked at the tree.

It was not very tall.

It was not very fat.

And it was a tiny bit crooked.

"I like it," said Oliver.

"A tree with a nest

makes me smile inside."

"Me too," said Mother.

"At last," said Father,

"we have found our Christmas tree."

Father chopped down the tree.

He and Oliver carried it home.

Amanda walked in Father's footsteps,

very carefully

carrying the nest.

FAT COOKIES

Outside it was snowing.

Inside Mother and Oliver and Amanda
were making cookies.

24

Mother rolled out the dough.

Oliver and Amanda used cookie cutters

to make shapes:

stars and bells and wreaths

and Christmas trees.

They put sprinkles on top

and popped them in the oven to bake.

They made three plates of cookies.

"I am tired of trees," said Oliver.

"The points of my stars

keep falling off," said Amanda.

"I have an idea," said Mother.

"Why don't you make your own

cookie shapes?"

"Oh, boy," said Oliver.

"I am going to make a snowman."

"I will make a reindeer," said Amanda.

Mother put away the cookie cutters.

Oliver took a ball of dough.

He smashed it flat.

"That is my snowman's head," he said.

"And that is his body."

"What a big snowman," said Mother.

"I like my cookies big," said Oliver.

He started making a Santa.

Amanda was working on her reindeer.

"Your reindeer looks like

an elephant," said Oliver.

Amanda started over again.

"Why does your reindeer have

a tree on its head?" asked Oliver.

"That's its antlers," said Amanda.

"Why does your Santa have a tail?"

"That's his bag of toys," said Oliver.

Jasmine
x

After she finished her reindeer

Amanda made a Christmas rabbit.

Oliver made a snowman family.

"These are beautiful cookies,"

said Mother.

She popped them in the oven to bake.

While they waited for their cookies,

Oliver and Amanda watched

the snow coming down.

Mother opened the oven door.

"What happened?" asked Amanda.

"My reindeer is all fat."

"All our cookies are fat,"

said Oliver. "They are ruined."

Mother looked at the cookies.

"I still think they are beautiful,"

she said. "You made them yourselves."

"Anyway, Santa should be fat.

And so should a snowman."

"A reindeer could be fat,"

said Amanda, "if he ate too much."

Outside the snow kept coming down.

Inside Mother and Oliver and Amanda

sat at the kitchen table,

eating warm cookies and milk.

"Will you have a fat cookie?"

asked Mother.

"They are too beautiful to eat,"

said Oliver.

"Let's save them to show Father."

So Mother had a bell.

And Oliver had a Christmas tree.

And Amanda had a star

with the points broken off.

"This is the part I like the most,"

said Oliver,

"about making Christmas cookies."

STOCKINGS

It was the day before Christmas.

The Christmas tree was up.

The stockings were hung

by the chimney, ready for Santa.

The packages were almost all wrapped.

Oliver had finally finished
his letter to Santa.
It was four pages long.

"How many things did you ask for?"
asked Amanda.
"Twenty-two," said Oliver.
"And they are all toys."
"Santa is not going to bring you
twenty-two toys," said Amanda.
"He might," said Oliver.

Amanda went to her room

to wrap more packages.

Oliver looked at his stocking.

"This stocking is not big enough

for a fire truck and a football

and a storybook and six new games,"

he said. "I think I need a new one."

Oliver went to the coat closet.

He saw the warm socks

that Father wore for shoveling snow.

"That is better," he said.

He hung up one of Father's socks.

"But it might not be big enough

for a dump truck and a doctor kit

and a giant talking teddy bear."

Oliver went back to the closet.

He couldn't find any more stockings.

But he saw his long stocking cap.

"A stocking cap is even better

than a stocking," he said.

He hung up the stocking cap.

"But it might not be big enough
for a bulldozer and a baseball bat
and a Super-duper Double-decker
Parking Garage."
Oliver went to his room.
He saw the pillowcase on his bed.
"That is much better," he said.
He hung up the pillowcase.

"Still it might not be big enough

for a steam shovel and a space suit

and a Mighty Midget Jet-powered

Motorcycle."

Oliver went all around the house.

He saw the dining room tablecloth.

"This might be big enough," he said.

He tied it up

and hung it up by the chimney.

"What is that?" asked Amanda.

"My new stocking," said Oliver.

"You can't do that," said Amanda.

"That is our Christmas tablecloth."

"Why is it so big?" asked Father.

"So Santa can bring me

twenty-two toys," said Oliver.

"My, oh, my," said Father.

"Do you really need twenty-two toys?"

"I don't need them," said Oliver.

"I just want them."

There was a knock on the door.

"Merry Christmas!"

It was Grandmother,

her arms full of packages.

"All of these are for tomorrow,"
she said. "Except this one."

"Christmas stockings!" said Oliver.
"I knitted them myself,"
said Grandmother.

"What nice stockings!" said Amanda.

"Nice and big," said Oliver.

And the two of them hung up

their new stockings

by the chimney, ready for Santa.

CHRISTMAS MORNING

"Wake up," said Oliver and Amanda.

"It's Christmas!"

Oliver pulled the covers off

of Mother and Father.

Amanda got their bathrobes,

and they all went downstairs

to see if Santa had come.

"He came!" said Oliver.

"I knew it," said Amanda.

"I heard reindeer up on the roof."

Oliver and Amanda opened

their stockings.

Oliver found a fire truck and a book

and a magic set in his stocking.

He shook it,

but nothing else came out.

Amanda found a paint set and a puzzle

and a baby doll.

"This is Patsy Ann," she said.

"She is too little to do anything.

But I will take care of her."

"Time for breakfast," said Mother.

They had piles of Christmas pancakes.

Amanda fed Patsy Ann from her plate.

Oliver parked his fire truck

next to his juice.

"If anything catches on fire,"

he said, "I am ready."

After breakfast

everyone put on Christmas clothes.

"How about some singing?"

said Grandmother.

Father played the piano

and they all sang Christmas songs.

Amanda rocked Patsy Ann in her arms.

Oliver put out a fire under the piano.

Then Father said, "I can't wait

a minute longer to find out

what is in all those packages."

"Me neither," said Oliver.

Father put on his Santa suit

and handed out the packages.

Everyone opened their gifts.

"Just what I wanted," said Mother
to Amanda. "A picture of you."
"Just what I needed," said Father
to Oliver. "A board with nails."
"It's to hang things up on,"
said Oliver.

"Thanks for the hats," said Oliver
and Amanda to Grandmother.
"I knitted them myself,"
said Grandmother.

Finally only two packages were left
under the Christmas tree.
Both of them were big.
"My bike!" said Amanda.
"My Mighty Midget Motorcycle!"
said Oliver.
They rode around and around
until they were all tired out.

"Oliver," said Father.

"I am sorry that Santa

did not bring you twenty-two toys."

"That's all right," said Oliver.

"I have enough."

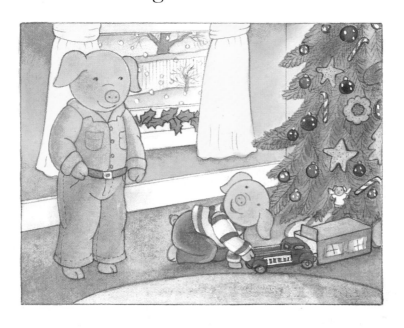

He parked his fire truck

in his new parking garage.

ALAMEDA FREE LIBRARY

Then he and Amanda put on

their new hats

and went outside to play in the snow.